W9-CRI-728

Barbie
GOES TO A PARTY

Story by JEAN BETHELL

Pictures by CLAUDINE NANKIVEL

WONDER BOOKS

1107 Broadway, New York 10, N. Y.

© 1964, by Mattel, Inc.
All rights reserved under International
and Pan-American Copyright Conventions.
Published simultaneously in Canada.
Printed in the United States of America.

"BARBIE" and "MIDGE" are the registered trademarks
of Mattel, Inc. for its TEEN-AGE DOLLS.
Used under license from Mattel, Inc.

"Hello?

Yes, this is Barbie."

"Hi, Barbie!

This is Nancy."

"Hi, Nancy! What's new?"

"I'm going to have a party.
Can you come?"

"Oh, yes, I'd love to!
Thank you very much!"

11

"Mother! Mother!
I'm going to a party!"

"That's nice, dear.

What will you wear?"

"Let me see.

I could wear this . . .

Or this . . .

Or this . . .

What do you think?"

15

"How about this?"

"Oh, no — that's too young."

"How about this?"

"Oh, no—that's too old."

"Do you like this?"

"No, dear."

"This one?"

"Not for a party."

"I like this dress."

"So do I.

You look very nice."

"But I can't wear it
to Nancy's party."

"Why not?"

"I wore it to JANE'S party!"

"Umm-m-m! Good!"

"It's for you, dear."

"Hello?

Yes, this is Barbie."

"Hi, Barbie!

This is Sue."

"Hi, Sue! What's new?

Are you going to Nancy's party?"

"Oh, yes!

Are you?

What are you going to wear?"

"I don't know, Sue.

What are YOU going to wear?"

"I don't know.

That's why I called you."

"Well, I'll call you back."

"All right, Barbie.

Good-by."

"That was Sue.
She doesn't know
what to wear."

"You don't say!"

"Hello!

May I come in?"

"Hello, Midge. How are you?"

"Hi, Midge!
Are you going to the party?"

"Yes. Are you, Barbie?

What are you going to wear?"

"I don't know.

What are YOU going to wear?"

"How about this?"

"Midge, I LIKE it!"

"Mother, do you like it?"

"It's very nice, dear.

But not for a party."

"She's right, Midge.

Not for a party."

"But what IS right for a party?"

"I don't know!

I'll call Nancy."

"Hi, Nancy!

This is Barbie."

"Hi, Barbie! What's new?"

"What shall we wear
to your party?"

"Wear ANY old thing.

It's going to be a picnic!"

"A picnic! Hooray!"

"Mother, it's going to be a picnic!
Now I know what we can wear!"

"I'll call the other girls."

"This is fun!

What a picnic, Nancy!"

"Midge, you look very nice."

"Thank you, Sue. So do you."

"I think Nancy looks nice."

"And so does Barbie."

"Let's pick the best-dressed girl!"

"All right. Who is she?"

"I pick Sue."

"I pick Nancy."

"I think it's Barbie."

"Oh, no, it's Midge."

"You're right, Sue."

"You're right, Midge."

"And so are you, Nancy."

"The best dressed girl is . . .

CHOOSE FROM THESE EASY READERS

5901 Will You Come to My Party?
5902 Hurry Up, Slowpoke
5903 Mr. Pine's Mixed-up Signs
5904 The Adventures of Silly Billy
5905 The Secret Cat
5906 Billy Brown Makes Something Grand
5907 Miss Polly's Animal School
5908 The Duck on the Truck
5909 A Train for Tommy
5910 Surprise in the Tree
5911 The Monkey in the Rocket
5912 Billy Brown: The Baby Sitter
5913 Fly-Away at the Air Show
5914 Arty the Smarty
5915 The Surprising Pets of Billy Brown
5916 Barney Beagle
5917 I Made a Line
5918 Laurie and the Yellow Curtains
5919 Grandpa's Wonderful Glass
5920 Benjamin in the Woods
5921 Barney Beagle Plays Baseball
5922 The Day Joe Went to the Supermarket
5923 Question and Answer Book
5924 Jokes and Riddles
5925 Let Papa Sleep!
5926 The Surprise in the Story Book
5927 The Big Green Thing
5928 The Boy Who Fooled the Giant
5929 More Jokes and Riddles
5930 Too Many Pockets
5931 The Clumsy Cowboy
5932 Cat in the Box
5933 How the Animals Get to the Zoo
5934 The Birthday Party
5935 Little Gray Mouse and the Train
5938 One Kitten is not Too Many
5939 How To Find a Friend
5940 The Boy, the Cat and the Magic Fiddle
5946 Barbie Goes to a Party